# Thank you for your Friendship

by Marianne Richmond

# Thank you for your Friendship

© 2004 by Marianne Richmond Studios, Inc.

All rights reserved. No part of this book may be reproduced or transmitted in any form or by any means, electronic or mechanical, including photocopying, recording or any information storage and retrieval system, without permission in writing from the publisher.

Marianne Richmond Studios, Inc.
420 N. 5th Street, Suite 840
Minneapolis, MN 55401
www.mariannerichmond.com

ISBN 0-9741465-4-4

Illustrations by Marianne Richmond

Book design by Sara Dare Biscan

Printed in China

Second Printing

TO

FROM

Date

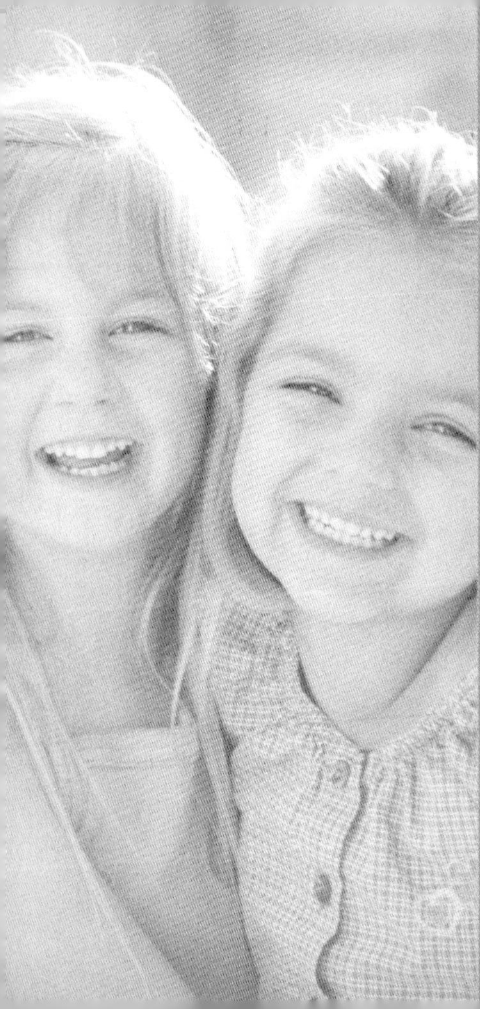

Thank you
for your
friendship.

I'm so glad
our paths crossed
along the way,
and that we both
recognized a friend
in the other...
because I can't
imagine not having
you in my life.

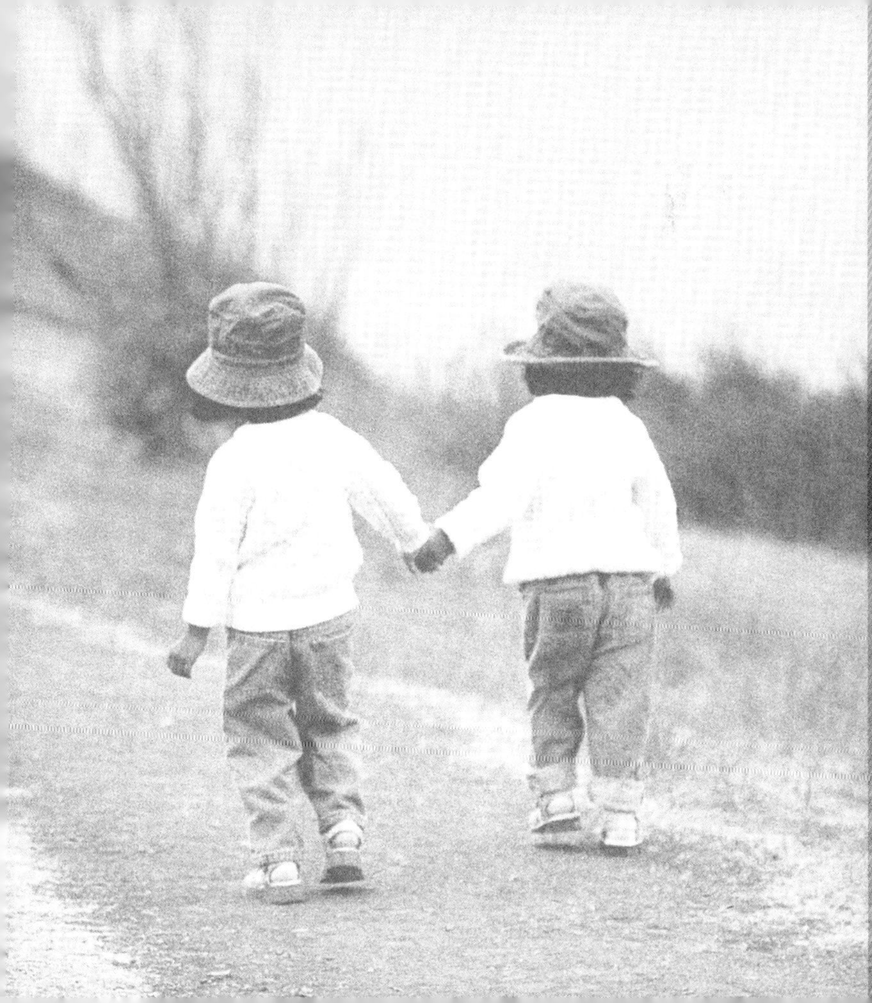

I'm grateful for
the way I can
just be myself
around you.

I can be silly
    or serious
or joyful
    or quiet...
and any mood is
okay with you.

Thanks for accepting that my very crabby mood is just one <u>itty</u> <u>bitty</u> part of the greater, lovable me.

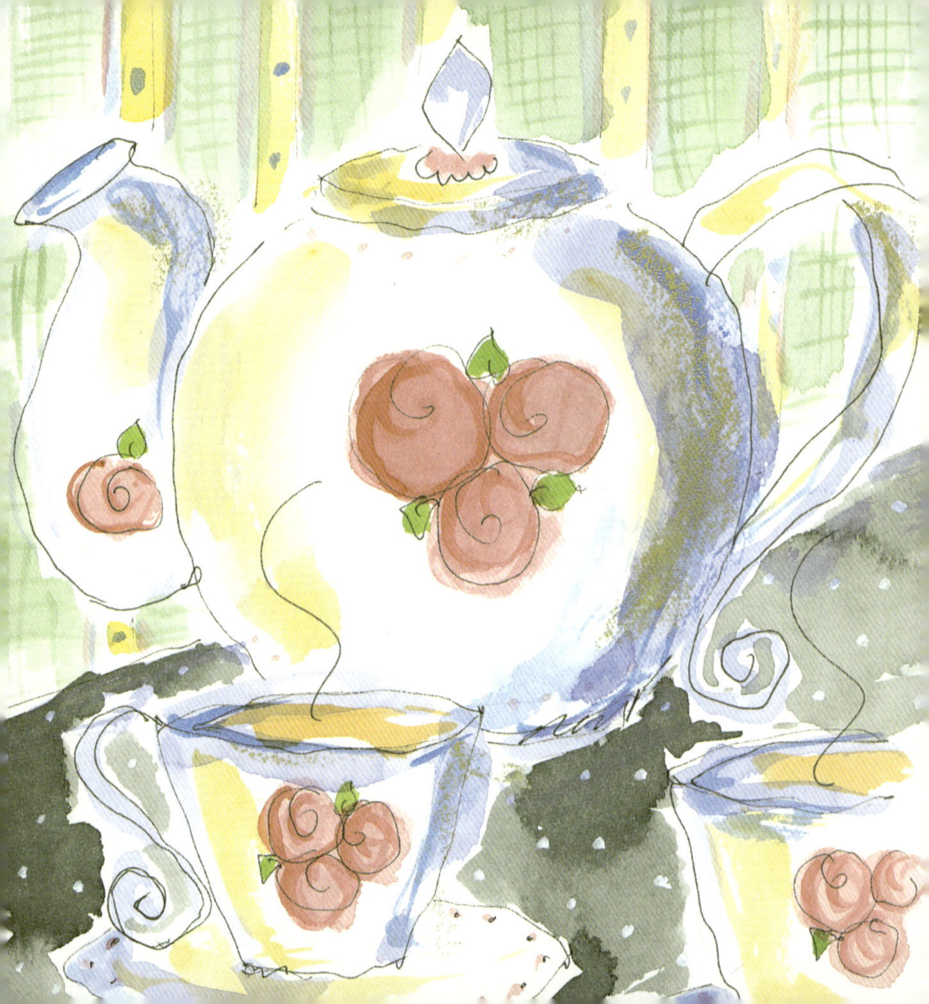

Thank you for being
a safe place for
my thoughts and feelings.

Thanks for listening to me,
understanding me,
and for not judging me.

Thanks for your

hopes for me.

I absolutely love laughing with you.
I'm amazed how we can crack
each other up with our
own brand of humor.

I think there are probably
lots of other people
who don't think
we're that funny.

Just so you know...
you ARE funny.

Thanks especially for encouraging me when I'm not feeling very brave... or capable... or successful.

You help me see the positive, and I need that.

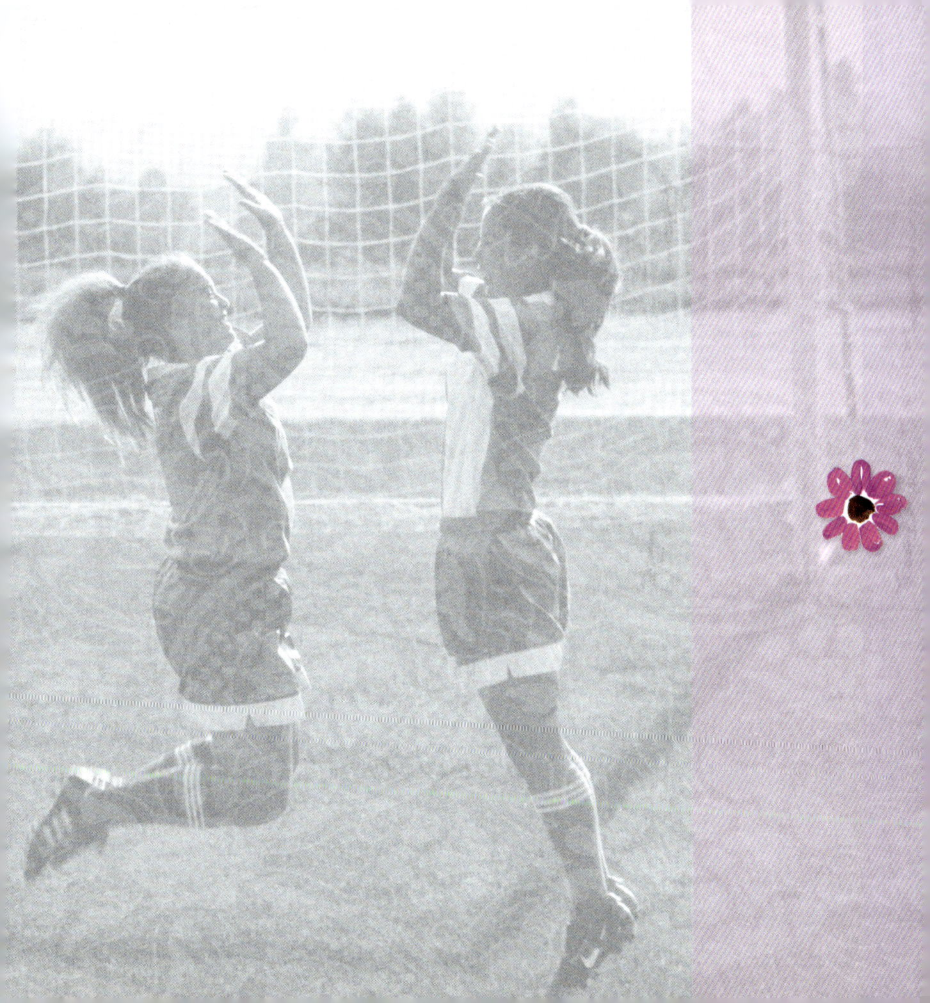

I feel so fortunate to know that you'll be there for me...

even if it's not-so-great timing for you.

You're a true,

"two-in-the-morning" friend,

though I'll try not

to need you then.

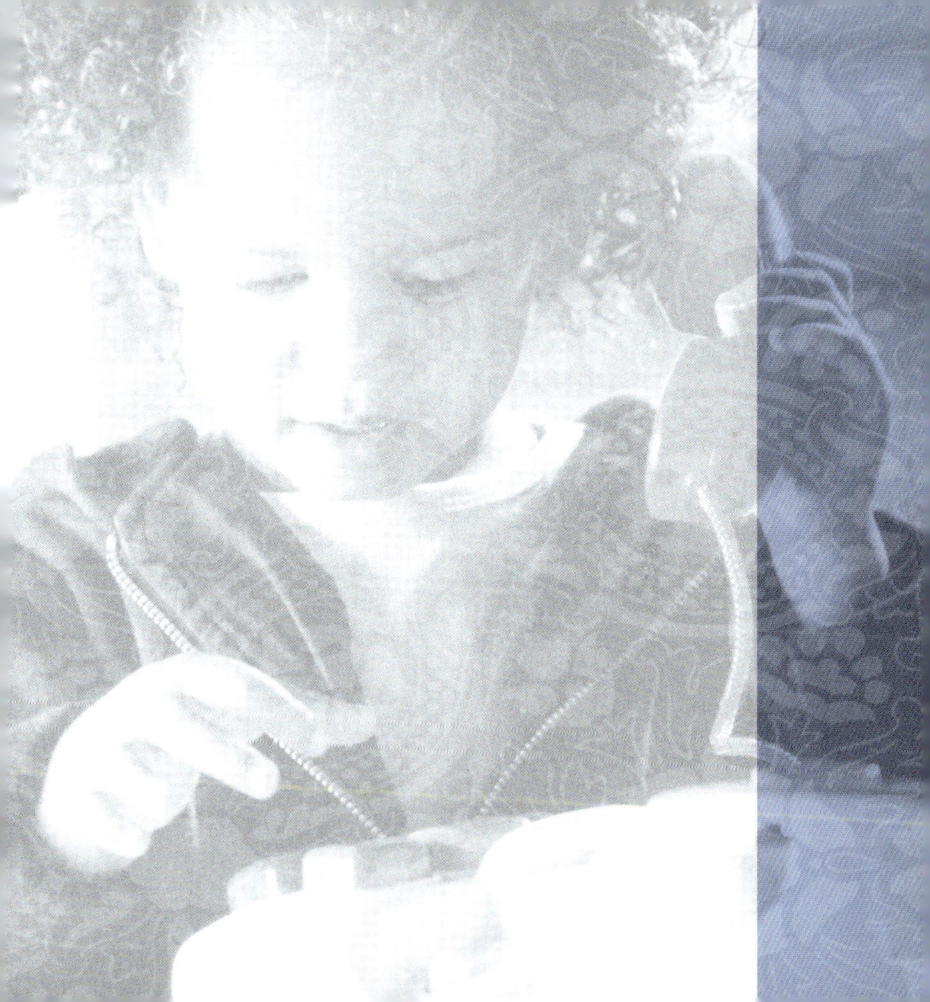

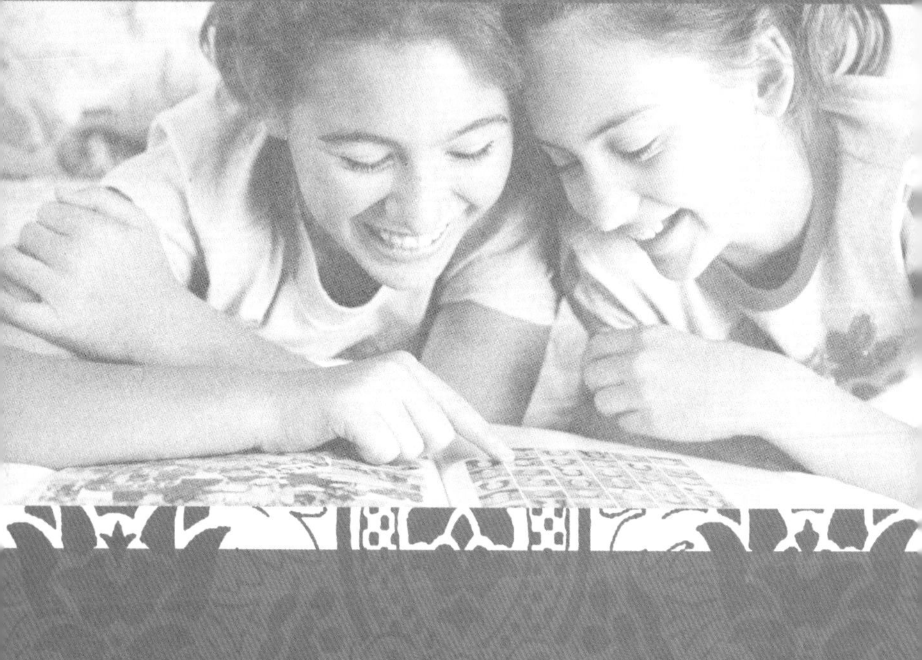

I like creating the story of our friendship... knowing each other long enough to have history, memories, inside jokes and genuine concern for the daily-ness of each other's life.

Thanks for your gentle honesty
 about my hair color,
the perceived size of my butt
 in my favorite jeans,
the best swimsuit for my shape,
 and if I should really level
with my boss.

(No need to be _as_ honest when I ask you if you like my guy or my mom.)

Thank you for keeping
  our friendship a priority
amidst jobs and families
  and commitments and life.

I need you for balance,
  perspective, support,
and comic relief.

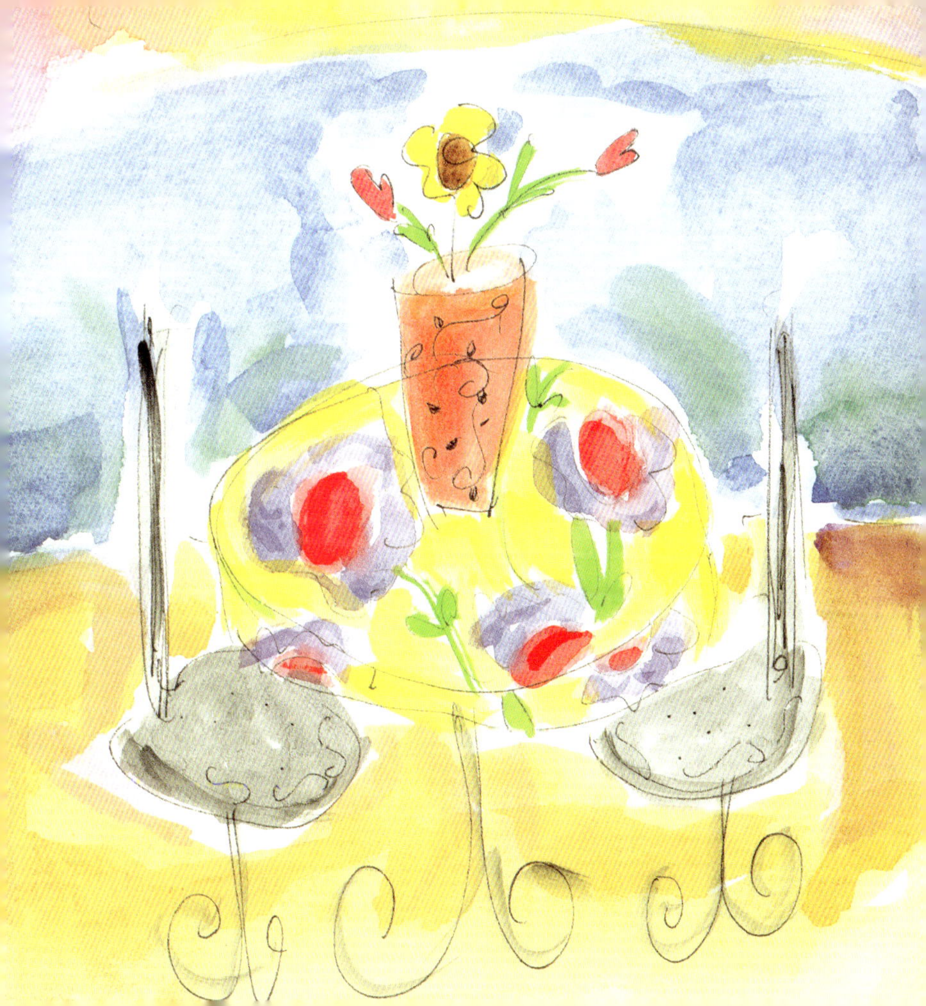

Someone told me that
if you go through life with
one or two best friends...

you are infinitely blessed.

I thought,

"how hard can <u>that</u> be?"

But as I go along,
I get it.

I realize more
and more how
very precious is
the gift
of friendship.

I realize what a treasure it is to find a friend who cares for me as much as I care for her.

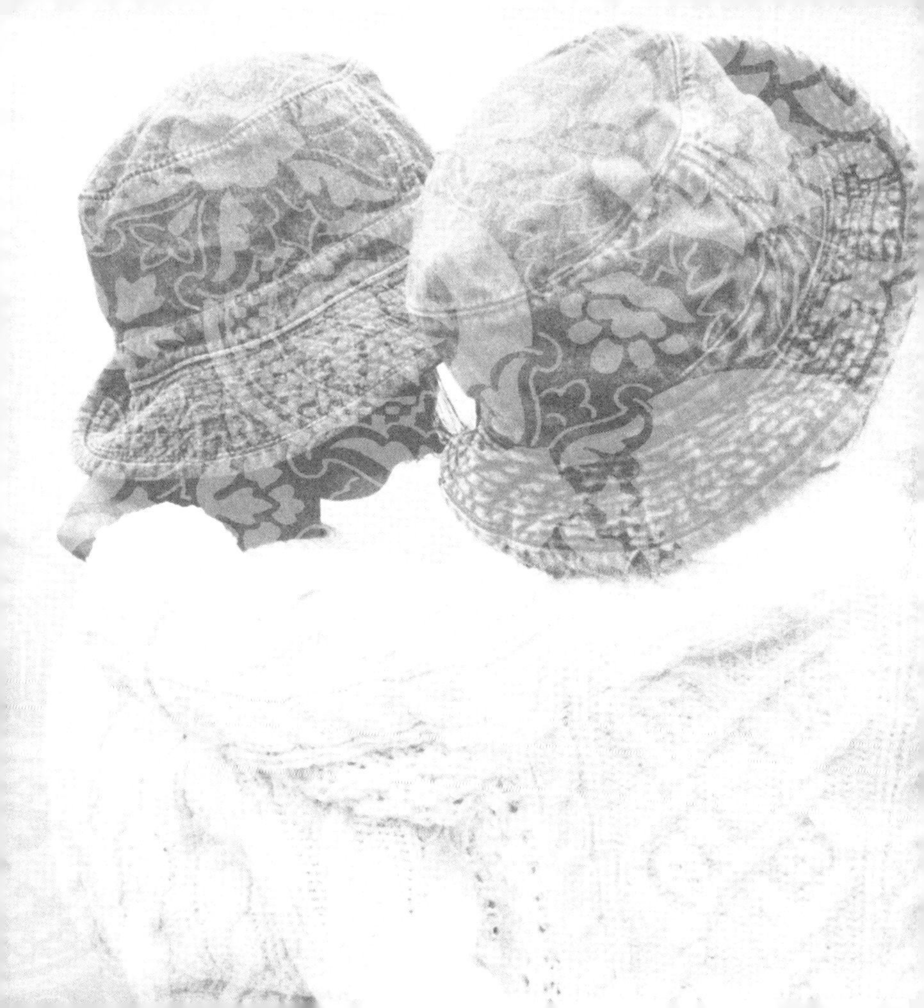

And I realize more and more that one real, honest, trustworthy, dependable friend is better than a hundred acquaintances.

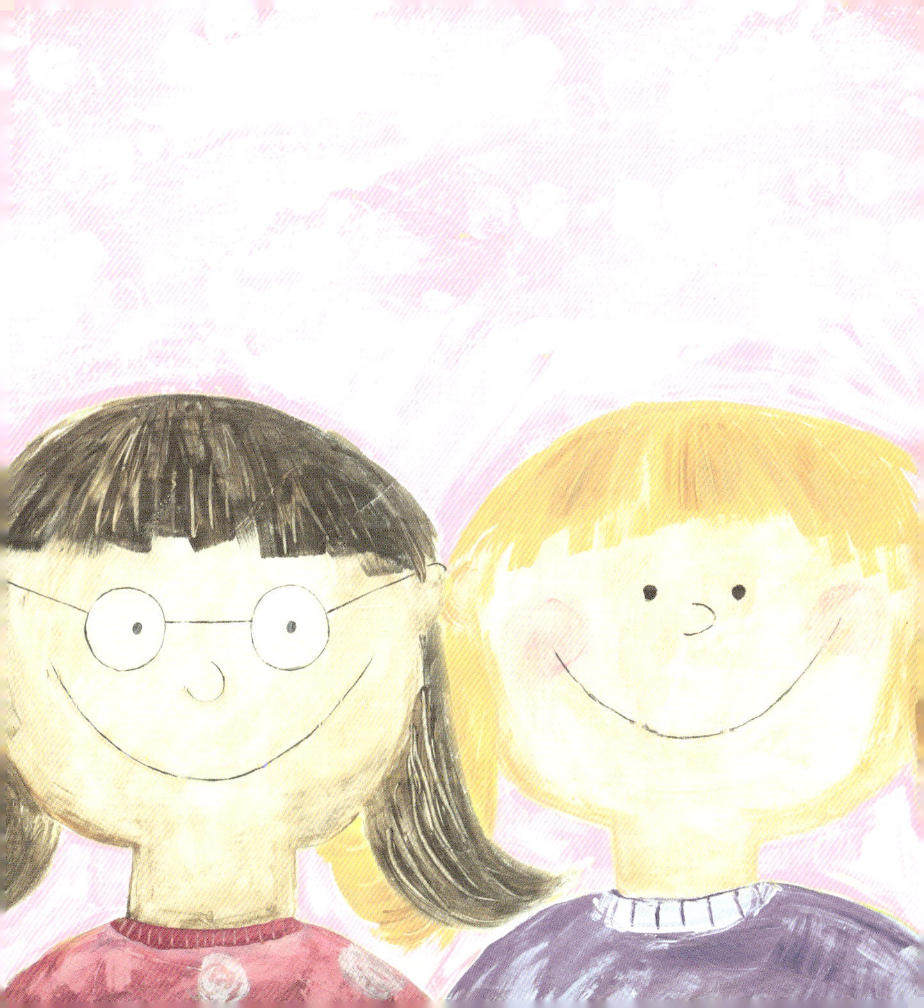

Thank you
for being
that kind
of friend.
You truly mean
the world
to me.

A gifted author and artist, Marianne Richmond shares her creations with millions of people worldwide through her delightful books, cards, and giftware. In addition to the *Simply Said...* gift book series, she has written and illustrated four additional books: **The Gift of an Angel, The Gift of a Memory, Hooray for You!** and **The Gifts of Being Grand.**

To learn more about Marianne's products, please visit www.marianunerichmond.com.